THE LAPSNATCHER

Story by Bruce Coville • Pictures by Marissa Moss

BridgeWater Books

For Orion and Cara
Been there, done that, lived to tell the tale. —B.C.

For Elias, who is a terrific big brother. —M.M.

Library of Congress Cataloging-in-Publication Data

Coville, Bruce.
The lapsnatcher / by Bruce Coville; pictures by Marissa Moss.
p. cm.
Summary: After he talks with an adult who was once a lapsnatcher, Jacob begins to feel differently about his new baby sister.
ISBN 0-8167-4233-2 (lib. bdg.)
[1. Sibling rivalry–Fiction. 2. Jealousy–Fiction. 3. Babies–Fiction. 4. Brothers and sisters–Fiction.] I. Moss, Marissa, ill. II. Title.
PZ7.C8344Lap 1997
[E]–dc20

96-21611

Once there was a little boy named Jacob who had a new baby sister. He did not like her very much.

The baby was two weeks old, and she got everything
Jacob wanted. She got her breakfast when he wanted his.
She got to make more noise than he was *ever* allowed to.
She got to sit in her swing and play while he was forced
to set the table for supper.

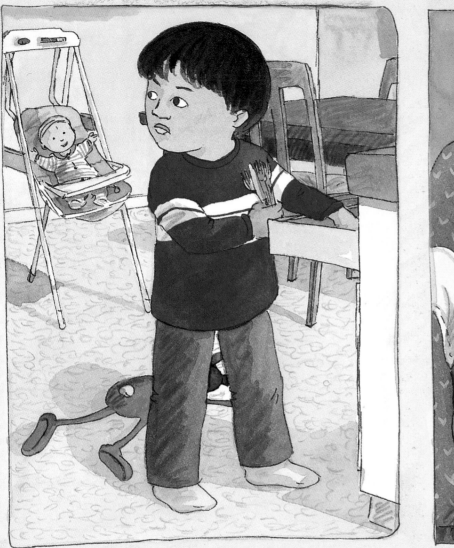

Worst of all, she got his mother's lap when he wanted to sit in it.

When his mother was pregnant, Jacob had thought having a sister would be fun. What a mistake!

Even then the baby had made things hard for him.

First, his mother had gotten so big around the middle that he couldn't fit into her lap anymore.

Then she had gone to the hospital to have the baby and there had been no lap for him at all.

And now that his mother had a lap again, the baby was always in it!

"That baby is a lapsnatcher," said Jacob.

"But we still love you just as much," said his mother.

"Then how come you don't play with me as much?"

"Because taking care of a brand-new baby is a lot of work. I have to feed her and change her and keep her things clean. I play with you as much as I can. I wish that I could play with you more."

"That baby is a lapsnatcher," said Jacob.
"But we still love you just as much," said his father.
"Then how come you don't play with me as much?"
"Because I have to help your mother more now. There are a lot of new jobs when a baby comes, more than Mommy can do by herself. That is why I am cooking supper instead of playing with you."

"That baby is a lapsnatcher," said Jacob.

"But we still love you just as much," said his grandmother.

"Then how come you are always bringing the baby new things and you hardly ever do that for me?"

"But I did when you were a baby," said his grandmother. "Besides, just yesterday I brought you a brand-new T-shirt, with a picture of a dinosaur on the front."

"That baby is still a lapsnatcher," said Jacob to himself.

Finally Jacob decided that he had better do something about this lapsnatcher.

One day when his mother was nursing the baby, Jacob was sitting on the steps outside his house. He saw the mailman coming up the street, and he had an idea.

When the mailman got there, Jacob said, "If I give you a stamp, will you mail my baby sister to Alaska?"

"Why do you want me to do that?" asked the mailman.

"Because she's a lapsnatcher!"

"A lapsnatcher?" asked the mailman. "Oh—I know what you mean. I had a baby sister who stole my favorite laps when I was little, too!"

"You did?" asked Jacob.

"You bet I did. And I really hated her for a while. But when she got older, she started to be more fun. I learned how to make her laugh. I could make her laugh better than anyone. I even started to like her some after a while."

"That's nice," said Jacob. "But I would still like to send *my* sister to Alaska."

"Aren't you afraid she might get eaten by a polar bear?"

"I suppose that could happen," Jacob sighed. "I'd better find somewhere else to send her."

The next day when Jacob's mother was changing the baby's diaper, the garbageman came.

"Wait!" called Jacob. "Would you please take my sister to the dump?"

"Why do you want me to do that?" asked the garbageman.

"Because she makes a lot of messes! Besides, she's a lapsnatcher."

"A lapsnatcher?" asked the garbageman. "Oh—I know what you mean. I had a baby brother who was a lapsnatcher when I was little!"

"A brother?" asked Jacob. He was surprised. He thought only sisters were lapsnatchers.

"You bet. Boy, was I mad when they brought *him* home. But when he got older, he turned out to be kind of fun. He used to dump his cereal on his head. I almost fell off my chair laughing. Did he ever look silly!"

"That's nice," said Jacob. "But I would still like to send *my* sister to the dump."

"Aren't you afraid someone might throw eggshells and coffee grounds on her head?" asked the garbageman.

"I suppose that could happen," sighed Jacob. "I'd better find somewhere else to send her."

The next day when his mother was taking a nap, the lady who drove the diaper service truck came to the door with a new delivery.

"Would you please take my sister back to the diaper place with you?" asked Jacob.

"Why?" asked the diaper lady. "Is she a lapsnatcher?"

The boy looked at her in surprise. "How do you know about lapsnatchers?"

"Simple. I used to be a lapsnatcher myself."

"You did?" asked Jacob.

"Yes, and I can tell you, my big brother really hated me for a while. But when I got bigger, I started to be more fun. He learned how to make me laugh. He began to show me how to do things. After a while, we got to like each other. Now he's just about my best friend in the whole world."

"I see," said Jacob. But that was all he said.

When Jacob's mother finished her work that day,
he asked if he could sit in her lap.
"Of course you may," she said.
He snuggled in.

"Do you think I'll ever be able to make the baby laugh?" he asked.

"When she gets a little older you will. You'll probably be her favorite person."

He thought about that for a minute.

"Will I be able to teach her things?"

"She'll learn more from you than from anyone."

"Will she ever dump a bowl of cereal on her head?"

"I expect so," said his mother, making a funny face. "I know you used to."

The boy laughed. Then he made his mother
tell him about all the things he had done when
he was a baby. His favorite story was about the
time he put underwear on his head.

"How long will it take for our baby to get older?" he asked at last.

"Oh, not too long," said his mother. "She gets a little older every day. She gets a little stronger and a little smarter and can do a little more for herself each day. And that gives me more time for you."

"Good!" said Jacob.

He was quiet for a minute. At last he said, very softly, "I guess
maybe we can keep that lapsnatcher."

"Good," whispered his mother, giving him a great big hug. "Let's."

And they did.